Little Stories for Big Hearts

Amanda Lee

Amanda

Little Stories for Big Hearts: Six Stories to Increase a Child's Emotional Intelligence
First Edition 2023
Copyright © 2023 by Amanda Lee

To order additional books:
www.amazon.com
www.mymommytheartist.com

ISBN: 978-1-952943-19-5

E-book Also Available
E-BOOK ISBN: 978-1-952943-21-8

Editorial & Book Packaging: Inspira Literary Solutions, Gig Harbor, WA www.inspiralit.com
Illustrations: Aldila Permata
Book Design: Brianna Showalter, Ruston, WA
Printed in the USA

This seat belongs to: _____

To M, E, and K:

You are the three reasons I wrote this book.

To the Adult Reader

My mission and purpose for writing this book was born when my own heart was shattered. During this difficult time, I doodled to express my pain and the lessons I learned from the heartache. My daughter asked me about one of my doodles one day, and as I began weaving the doodle into a story to help her understand, I was pleasantly surprised as I realized that she was fully comprehending a complex concept about having boundaries. My desire to teach my kids more of these concepts ignited something inside of me, and these little stories began pouring out of me. This storybook is a compilation of a few of those efforts.

It has brought me the greatest joy and healing to watch my pain transform into the creation of a gift from my big heart to kids with big hearts everywhere. My hopes are that this book encourages connection between children and adults, and encourages genuine conversation about life's most important lessons. May these stories help you explain vital concepts of emotional health and intelligence, which might not have been taught when we were young: self-love, respect, empathy, intuition, building and keeping strong boundaries, and how healthy friendships should look and feel.

Just as the panda will remind you: may you and your children always remember you are deserving of love and kindness, from others and—most importantly—from yourselves.

Hi there, friend, come have a seat!
I'm glad you're here to read with me!

This book is so special, just like you,
it's all about kids and what they feel too.

So, whether you're having an up or down day,
sit with me and turn the page!

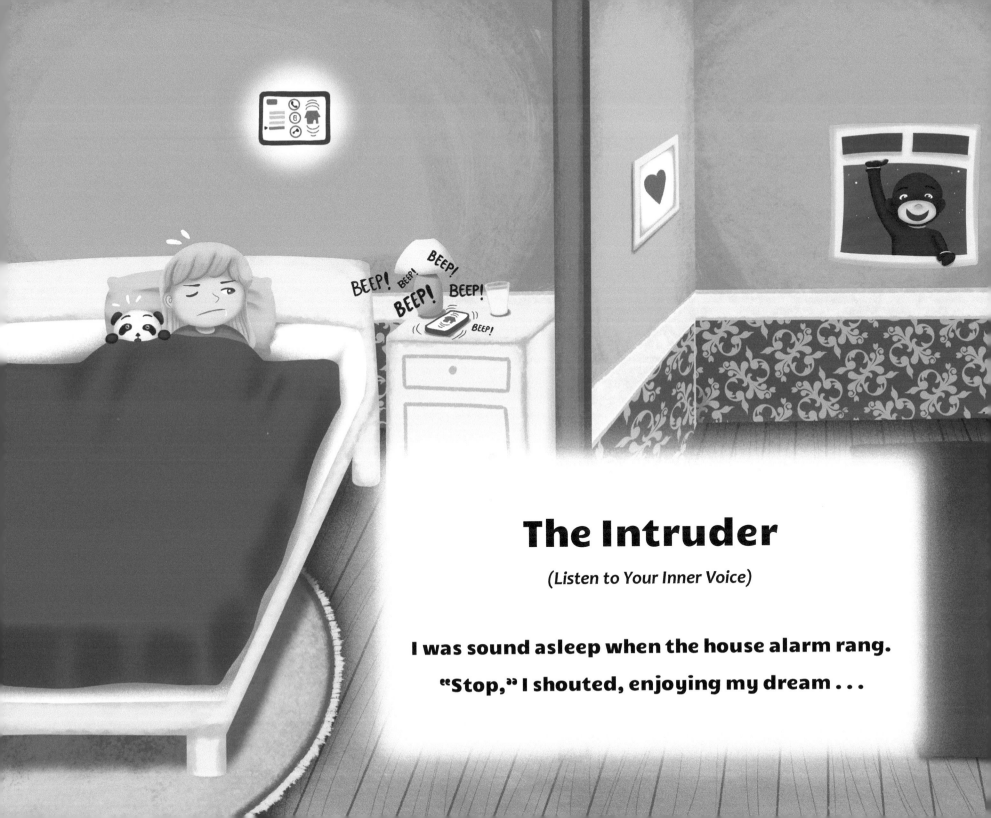

The Intruder

(Listen to Your Inner Voice)

I was sound asleep when the house alarm rang.

"Stop," I shouted, enjoying my dream . . .

. . . of turtles in spaceships and skating in space,
with ice cream cones sprinkling around me like rain.

Would you blame yourself, and question your choices?

"I shouldn't have bought this; it makes all these noises!"

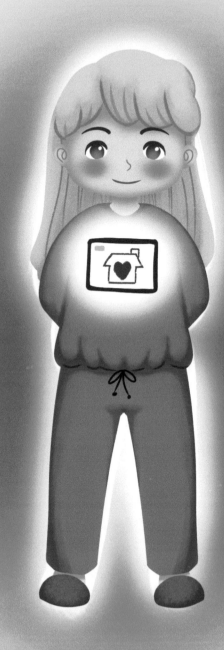

We all have an alarm, deep inside each of us–
a warning system, a feeling that we can trust.
It helps us along in decisions we make;
just like an alarm, it helps keep us safe!

So, when you hear an alarm going off in the night
or a sense in your body that "something's not right,"
you should always listen and not think it's teasing–
that funny feeling is there for a reason!

It takes practice to trust our inner alarm,

but it's certainly worth it, to keep us from harm.

Just like drawing or dancing or making music:

we get better at it the more that we do it!

Hey, look over there! Do you see what I see?

I see something orange; what could that be?

Let's read the next story in our little book

. . . turn the page and take a look!

What's That, behind the Fence?

(Don't Judge Others Too Quickly)

What is that orange thing behind the fence?

Think about it; do you have a guess?

Is it a kid walking by,
giving a basketball a spin?

Or maybe it's neither, and what's there instead
is a rollerblading monster with a hat on its head!
When a tiny piece of the picture is all I can see
I can't fully understand who or what it could be.

So, be gentle with others wherever you go –
there's more to a person than you'll ever know!

When we see a whole person, being kind becomes easy,

though sometimes it's hard and a little bit messy.

Speaking of kindness, we need to beware.

(Please listen closely to this panda bear.)

Kindness does not mean we let people hurt us.

People who don't admit fault can be dangerous!

This you will see in the very next story

of a crocodile who just won't confess and say sorry.

If someone won't apologize–blames everything on you . . .

Well, if this were *your* story, what would *you* do?

The Boy and the Crocodile

(Beware of Tricky People Who Always Blame Others)

I'll tell you a story; you're here just in time!

I was going to the market, which opened at nine

to sell my apples, from my big apple tree.

I've lovingly cared for my crop, you can see.

I was well on my way down a road lined with trees

when . . . BUMP!

A big crocodile ran into me!

"My apples, my apples–

Oh no, OH NO!"

"Hey," said the crocodile, "watch where you go!"

"Watch where *I* go?" I tried to ask kindly,

"The signs mark the way—*you* ran into *me!*"

"You must be mistaken," lied the large, green croc.

"*You* bumped into *me*; it's all *your* fault!"

"Actually," I said, to set the tale straight,
"you were walking the wrong way;
you saw me too late."

"So, you're calling *me* bad
and so very TERRIBLE?"
he yelled as he stomped
with a sound that was horrible.

"Tell me, how is it *I* who bumped into *you*?

When you and your apples bumped into me too?

Why did *you* not move out of the way?

If you were more careful, clear of me you would stay!

It's really *your* fault you left home with that fruit. If you cared for your apples, you'd be careful, wouldn't you?

"What are you doing? Why would you do this?

My beautiful fruit–my hard work–is now useless!"

"You should be thanking me for cleaning this stuff up.

Look around; I'm the only one fixing your mess-up!"

I feel so confused and so bad inside.

I wouldn't hurt anyone, not even a fly.

But the crocodile said that I ruined his day!?

He wouldn't be upset if I'd not been in his way.

Maybe he's right; what have I done?

Please tell me, friend, did I do something wrong?"

That story makes me feel a little sad,
frustrated, too, and a little bit mad.
The crocodile wouldn't admit his mistake.
He wouldn't say, "Sorry," for the trouble HE made.

Some people are like this; they never say sorry.

When that happens; you stick to your story!

When you meet those people who try to confuse:

remember who *you* are and stick to the truth.

It's true: who *you* are is a gift to this earth!

Now, read this next story to learn about worth . . .

The Lemonade Stand

(Believe in Yourself)

I gathered ingredients with Mom, at the store:

"Only two lemons? We need many more!"

I wanted to rush home because I was thrilled,

thinking of cup after cup I would fill.

I set up the stand; it was all nice and neat

and I called out to folks passing by on the street,

to people who'd traveled from far, distant lands:

"I'll bet you are thirsty! Come visit my stand!

If you've had a long day, well then step right on up!

I'll make your day better with only one cup!"

"If you're feeling down 'cuz your teddy is lost

Or maybe your favorite shirt's in the wash.

Maybe you lost your keys in a hole

or hungry raccoons stole your cinnamon roll!

No matter how bad your day might seem to be,

my lemonade will make it right—you'll see!"

Would you like to try some?
It cures everything!
It just tastes SO GOOD;
it might make you sing!

A customer walks up,
the first of the day!
I offer her lemonade,
but what does she say?
'No, thanks; I don't really
like lemonade–
I prefer apple juice,
but thanks anyway!'

WHAT DID SHE SAY? She won't even try?

Did I forget an important ingredient this time?

I followed my recipe (secret, of course);

I don't understand it—so hard I worked.

Maybe it doesn't taste as good as I thought it.

I can't believe she didn't want it!

Maybe I should stop, and give up my dream.

This wasn't the success I thought it would be!

"Excuse me, do you sell the best lemonade?

I've heard all about you and this drink that you've made!

I love lemonade and would like to try it . . .

I'm not sure I've ever had anything like it."

The boy takes a drink and says in a flash,

"This is the *best* lemonade I've had!"

"Really?" I ask. "It tastes okay?"

Yes!" he says. "This will fix any bad day!

I love it so much: I hope you'll make more!

I wish I could find it in every store!"

I guess not *everyone* will like what I make,
but that doesn't make it less yummy or great.
I'll keep on working to make what I make,
and be who I am, 'cuz who I am is GREAT!

There are many people, but only one you!

The world needs *all* of us to do what we do,

to listen to our hearts, to follow our dreams, to–

BLAGH! OOGY BOOGY, WAAA- EEE-!

What's that sound? Someone sounds upset!

Turn the page, to see what's up next!

The Emotions Factory

(Sorting out Our Big Feelings)

BLAGH, OOGY BOOGY, WAAAA—EEEEE—ROOOOO-SQUEEE!

I just crashed my bike and hurt my knee!

Since you're here, let me ask you if you've ever felt

like SQUAWBY DOO HONK BOO GREMELT!

My knee hurts; I don't know
what words I should use.
I feel too many things;
I don't know how to choose!
I'm not quite sure–
I might be hungry, too.
Trying to figure it out
makes me MORE confused!

I feel like there is a big hole in my tummy.

I bet everyone saw me; it makes me feel yucky.

I'm lonely and wish someone would give me a hug.

I don't know how to say it; I feel as small as a bug!

I'm scared like I'm running from one million bees
and no matter what I do, they all surround me!
I want to leap and do a big HIYAA!
–break a wood board or rip something up!

"Hello there!"

"These boxes of feelings–do you think you can help

me slow down these emotions moving down the belt?

I don't have the words, but I'm glad you are here.

Maybe we can sort through these feelings together!"

Understanding our feelings takes practice, I know.

I'm still learning how to do it too, so . . .

be patient with yourself when you feel frustrated

and find someone you love to help you get sorted.

Feelings are our bodies' way

to communicate messages that help us say

what we might need, and if we need help.

So look around; who can you tell?

Most importantly, what we need to do

is honor and love ourselves, to ourselves be true.

Be proud that you are the miracle you are.

There's none other like you—not near, not far!

As you grow up, you'll need to be kind

and try to keep other people's feelings in mind.

Treat others nicely–share and give.

Try to cheer others up, encourage and uplift.

Open your heart, and use "empathy."

(That means to think about other people's needs.)

Be gentle with others, wherever you go.

Then . . . there's one more important thing

I think you should know ...

House and Fence

(Choose Your Friends Wisely)

I invited a friend over to play with my toys
but she came to my house and only destroyed!
Even when I asked her, "Please, please stop!"
she ruined my toys without giving a thought.

"Why would you do that?!" I cried in dismay.

"How could you treat me and my things in this way?"

And when I decided she needed to leave

(she was hurting my feelings and breaking my things),

she got angry at me that I asked her to go.

I told her she hurt me, but she disagreed, "NO!"

It was then that I knew I had to decide

which people I'd allow to come visit inside.

If she doesn't show the respect that *she* wants,

is she a good friend I'd ask over a lot?

No!

After all . . .

Around our houses, we build a fence.

We really don't let just anyone in.

You put up a fence so you can choose

who can come over and play with you.

You love your house and pick every detail,
protect your possessions and toys, without fail.
You choose what's allowed there and what you remove;
no one else loves your house like you do.

So . . .

When you're asked to be kind; I hope you will choose
to listen to your heart and inner voice too.
Since you love your house, who you are, what you do,
you should only allow people who respect those things too!

Thank you, my friend, for reading with me.

Did you read one story? Or two or three?

You might be experiencing lots of feelings

and feel like you could burst through the ceiling!

Know this:

You deserve to be loved whether you feel up or down

'specially on days when you just want to frown,

also on days when your smile is wide

and you feel like you're soaring up high in the sky!

You are so special whether cheery or blue!

You should be so proud–you're uniquely you!

About the Author

Amanda Lee has worked with children for over 20 years as a piano teacher, preschool teacher, and the creator of a social-emotional art class. Her own journey of healing from emotional abuse fuels her mission to advocate for children and their emotional health.

Amanda's sixth-grade teacher told her she would be an author one day, and she has made that prediction into a reality through her books and teaching. Amanda's work as an author encapsulates the magic and charm that has allowed her to connect with children over the course of her 20 years as a music and art teacher.

Amanda lives with her husband and three children in Seattle, where she teaches music and art along with her writing. She is currently working on a Master's degree in psychology, with an emphasis on child development.

www.mymommytheartist.com

Acknowledgments

To my three children - When I stumbled while creating this book, it was your three big hearts that picked me back up and kept me going. The greatest honor I have is being your mom. Thank you for being the amazing humans that you are. I am forever grateful for each day I get the chance to know you, support you, and most importantly, love you. May this book always serve as a reminder of the kind of love I always believe you deserve, from others and from yourselves.

To my parents - Thank you for keeping every story I wrote, every project I made, and every little Post-it® note I scribbled on and left around the house during my childhood. You taught me that my creations are valuable, which gave me the confidence to write this book.

To my husband - You are proof that goodness still exists. Thank you for seeing me and loving me for exactly who I am. In doing so, you amplify my creativity and drive. Thank you for listening each time I write something new and excitedly interrupt whatever you're doing to tell you about it. Thank you for the endless discussions on philosophy, life, love, and how together we will help generations to come. Thank you for holding space for my fears and my pain and offering love and reassurance. Thank you for reminding me of who I am when I have moments of doubt. Thank you for always keeping my electronics charged, my laundry clean, my belly full, and for finding my things before I even have a chance to misplace them.

To my friends - Thank you for patiently listening to every one of my "Ted Talk rants" about advocating for children, at every get-together, on every walk, and at every girls' night out. Thank you for encouraging me to pursue what I feel called to do.

To my late grandfather- I will never forget when you told me: "You have the ability to accomplish anything you want." Look, I did it! Thank you for believing in me.

To Mr. Walters - When you were my teacher in Grade 6, you said, "I think you're going to be an author one day." The world needs more educators like you.

To my friend Pye - You looked me in the eye and said, "Why are you sitting on these stories and not sharing them with the world?" Your one question ignited the creation of this entire book. Thank you.

To Arlyn at Inspira - Thank you for holding my hand through the daunting process of publishing my first book. Thank you for your endless patience!

And lastly, but certainly not least…

To all the past versions of myself - Thank you for leading me here. Look at what we've overcome! Look at how many times we got back up, especially when it felt like we couldn't anymore. Look at what we've learned, and the lives we will touch because we never gave up.

CPSIA information can be obtained
at www.ICGtesting.com
Printed in the USA
LVHW070805020323
740629LV00001B/3